HITTY'S TRAVELS

#1

Civil War Days

ELLEN WEISS

ILLUSTRATED BY BETINA OGDEN

ALADDIN PAPERBACKS

New York   London   Toronto   Sydney   Singapore

First Aladdin Paperbacks edition September 2001
Text copyright © 2001 by Ellen Weiss
Illustrations copyright © 2001 by Betina Ogden

Aladdin Paperbacks
An imprint of Simon & Schuster
Children's Publishing Division
1230 Avenue of the Americas
New York, NY 10020

Designed by Debra Sfetsios
The text of this book was set in CelestiaAntiqua
Printed in the United States of America

2 4 6 8 10 9 7 5 3 1

Library of Congress Control Number 2001092388
ISBN 0-689-84671-1

CHAPTER ONE

What Nell Inherited

My name is Hitty, which is short for Mehitabel. I am made of wood. I came into being in the state of Maine, in the frozen winter of the year 1829. There, an old peddler carved me out of a mountain ash tree.

My first owner was a girl named Phoebe Preble. She loved me, dressed me, and cared for me for years. But nothing lasts forever. The day came when I had to part ways with Phoebe.

Since then, I have belonged to many different children. Life has brought me many adventures, both large and small. I would like to tell you about one of them now. It is a story of great joy and awful sadness. It is the tale of a friend-ship that could not be broken.

My story begins in a four-poster bed in the state of North Carolina. The year was 1859. I was lying in this bed beside my owner. Her name was Cornelia Cleopatra Davis. Everyone called her Nell for short. She had long blond hair and eyes as green as the Maine sea I missed so much.

Nell had received me as a birthday present a few months before. Her mother had found me in a shop in Baltimore, where she was visiting relatives. When Nell laid eyes on me, she hugged me *hard*. I was afraid my arms would come off! Now she slept with me every single night. She had no brothers or sisters, so I became the one to whom she told her secrets.

On this June night, the moon shone brightly over the South. Streaming through the lace curtains, the light made patterns on the sheets.

Nell had been sleeping soundly but suddenly, she was awakened by a noise.

"What was that, Hitty?" Nell whispered. I listened closely. Yes, there it was again! What could it be? It sounded like crying. And it was very nearby.

Nell grabbed me and sat up in bed, listening. The crying continued. It was soft, but it did not stop. It was in her own room! We were both frightened, I don't mind telling you.

The noise seemed to be coming from the foot of her bed. Carefully, Nell lit the candle at her bedside. She gathered up her nightgown. Slowly, she crawled to the end of the bed. Then she gasped.

There, at the end of the bed, was a small cot. And on the cot was a girl about her own age. The girl lay staring at the ceiling. Tears made tracks down her chestnut-colored cheeks. When the girl saw us hanging over the bed looking at her, she gasped too.

"Who are *you*?" asked Nell.

"My name is Sarina," replied the girl. "I done been given to you." Fresh tears poured from her eyes.

"Given to *me*? How can that be?"

The girl sat up. She wiped her cheeks with the sleeve of her rough cotton nightshirt. "I belonged to your grandmother, Miz Henrietta. She put it in her will that you were to have me. I'm going to belong to you now. To be just yours."

Now Nell was beginning to understand. Her grandmother had died about a month before. Nell was not sad about this. She had never met her grandmother, who lived far away in Natchez, Mississippi. But she must have left Sarina to Nell. In those days, slaves were property. When someone died, they were sold or handed down, just like money or paintings. Or dolls, for that matter.

Though the South was beautiful, I'd had some difficulty getting used to life there. The Maine I had come from was a very different place. There, the sea pounded the rocky shoreline. The winters were harsh. People there were as rugged as the land. They liked doing things by themselves.

The South had a much kinder climate. The hills were green and rolling. The weather was warm. It had good land for large farms, and the farms were worked by slaves.

Nell's father owned a farm. It was about a thousand acres, not very large for the South. It took about forty slaves to work the land. They grew cotton, tobacco, beans, and corn. Another few slaves worked in Nell's father's big white house.

In Maine, we did not have slaves. The idea of people owning other people was strange to me. I cannot say I liked it. It was difficult enough for me, a doll, to be passed from hand to hand. Sometimes I was treated well, sometimes not. I'd had owners who had forgotten to clothe me, or dropped me in puddles. But I was made of wood. For a live girl, I could not imagine how hard it could be, to belong to someone else.

"When did you get here?" Nell asked Sarina.

"Just about an hour ago," said Sarina. "They made me up this bed real quiet so as not to wake you."

Nell stared at Sarina. "But I don't want a slave!" she said. Nell was a strong-willed girl. She was used to doing things by herself.

"Well, you done got me."

Nell was wide awake by this time. "You *got* me," Nell corrected her. "Not 'you *done* got me.' If you're going to sleep in my room, you might as well speak correctly."

"Yes, miz," said Sarina.

"And don't call me 'miz,'" Nell added. "Call me Nell."

"Yes, Miz Nell."

Nell just sighed. "Let's go to sleep," she said. She blew out the candle.

In the morning, Sarina was still there. She was still staring at the ceiling. I didn't think she had slept a wink. The early morning light was thin and watery.

"You have to sleep sometime," Nell said to Sarina.

Sarina did not answer.

"Why are you so sad?" said Nell. "This is a nice place. You'll see."

"I had to leave my mother and my father. They got sold someplace else. Only my big brother Joseph came here with me."

"He did?" asked Nell. "Where is he?"

"Outside. He works in the fields."

"Oh," said Nell. She thought about this for a moment. "If I had to leave my mother and father, I'd be very sad," she said.

Sarina said nothing.

"But you're a slave, and slaves have to do it all the time. Maybe you don't mind so much," Nell continued.

I was rather shocked to hear Nell say these things. But then I had to remind myself that Nell had lived here all of her life. It was difficult even for an adult to think differently from those around her. Certainly, it was impossible for a child. In a hundred years, probably many of the things I myself believed would seem ridiculous.

Then she gave me one last hug, and held me out to Sarina. "This is Hitty," she said. "She's mine, but I'm giving her to you. Maybe she'll make you feel better."

Sarina looked at me, her eyes very big.

"Go ahead, take her," urged Nell.

Without a word, Sarina reached out and took me. She looked at me as if I were a star fallen from heaven. Turning me this way and that, she inspected me. She touched my hair, my red cotton dress, and my painted face.

"I made her dress myself," said Nell.

Carefully, Sarina lifted my dress and looked at my slip. My name was sewn onto it in red thread. It had been embroidered by Phoebe, my first owner.

After a long, long time, Sarina drew me toward her. She hugged me carefully, not the way Nell had. She seemed afraid to break me. She was hardly breathing at all.

I was happy to be Sarina's. I like to be useful, and the only way a doll can be useful is to let someone love her.

"I think Hitty likes you," said Nell.

CHAPTER TWO

Work

At eight o'clock sharp, the door opened. In bustled Angela. Angela was the head of the house slaves. She had belonged to the family for many years. She'd taken care of Nell ever since she was born. A large, plushy woman, she could still move fast. She missed nothing, and she ruled with a hand of iron. Angela had a son named Henry. He was sixteen. He worked in Mr. Davis's stables. I'd only seen Henry once.

Angela crossed the room and threw the curtains open. "Time to get out of those beds, you two," she said. "Time's wasting."

Then she looked down at Sarina and me. "I see young Hitty's found a new owner," she said. She didn't smile, but I could tell she was pleased.

Nell sat up and rubbed her eyes, while Sarina scrambled out of bed, still clutching me. Angela looked her up and down.

"What kind of work did you do at Twin Oaks, child?" she asked Sarina.

"Didn't have to work," said Sarina. "Miz Henrietta done said I could wait until I was nine to start. I'm still eight."

"Not *done* said. *Said*," Angela corrected her. "Maybe nobody took the time to teach you to speak correctly at Twin Oaks. But here you will learn."

"Yes'm," said Sarina.

"Now," said Angela. "About your clothes. I suppose you can wear the dress you have now for a while." She looked at the dress Sarina had come with. It had blue and white stripes. "When winter comes," Angela continued, "you will be given a new linsey-woolsey dress. For the summer you can go barefoot. We'll give you a pair of shoes when the cold weather comes."

"Yes'm," said Sarina. I could see her shudder a bit, and so did Nell. Nobody wanted to wear linsey-woolsey. It was coarse wool, and it scratched.

"You're a good girl," Angela said. "As long as you do what you're told, your life here will be all right. You should be thankful that you're not working out in the fields. Now get dressed, and I'll show you how to do your chores. You will fetch water, help prepare food, and wash dishes. You can kindle the fires, too. If there's time, you'll help me serve at the table. You'll also change the linens and get Nell whatever she wants. Understand?"

"Yes'm." Sarina looked a bit dazed.

"After today, you'll start working at six in the morning. You'll have to leave Hitty here while you're working," said Angela. "But when you've finished, you may play with Nell. She's an only child. She needs company."

Sarina held me close. I could tell she was afraid. She had so much to learn! And what would happen if she couldn't master all these chores? It made my head spin just to think about it. And she could not even keep me nearby for comfort.

"Now, get dressed," said Angela. "I'll see you downstairs in the kitchen in ten minutes. It's through the parlor and straight back."

"Yes'm."

Angela turned and left the room.

As soon as she was gone, Nell jumped onto Sarina's bed. "Don't be scared of her," Nell said. "She looks tough, but she's really soft as pudd'n."

Sarina did not speak. She was still fighting back tears as she hurried to get dressed.

"I'll bring Hitty downstairs with me," said Nell. "That way, you can see her, at least."

And so, the day began for both girls. Their days were very different. Nell went back to sleep for a little while. She was tired after the excitement of the night before. She knew Sarina was supposed to help her get dressed. But she didn't want any help.

Nell took me downstairs when she was dressed. She had some toast for breakfast. Then she practiced the piano for half an hour. She did not enjoy practicing. She didn't think she was very good at the piano. But a young lady was supposed to be able to play, at least a little.

At noon, her tutor arrived. His name was Mr. Randolph, and he was young and handsome. He taught Nell how to read, write, and do her sums. They also read things in French, which I found fascinating. But the whole time, I knew Nell was really thinking about what it would be like to grow up and marry Mr. Randolph. She knew that his first name was Douglas. *Mrs. Douglas Randolph.* That's what her name would be. She often whispered to me about Mr. Randolph, when no one was about. "He is only thirteen years older than me," she would say. "Maybe he'll wait till I grow up."

After luncheon, Nell carried me back up to her room. She wanted to do some work on her sewing sampler. Angela had taught her how to do cross-stitching. The sampler had all the ABC's, and all the numbers, too. Nell was already up to the letter Q. At the bottom there was a sentence. It said, "CHARITY BEGINS AT HOME."

Taking me over to the open window, she gazed out. The breeze felt good to me. It was already getting very hot.

Then something caught my eye in the yard below. It was Sarina. She was carrying a huge wooden bucket of water from the pump.

Though she tried not to spill it, the water sloshed out onto her bare feet.

"Oh, Hitty, it's so heavy!" Nell whispered.

As we watched, a gang of field slaves passed by outside. They were stopping work for lunch. A young man with powerful muscles leaned over the fence and called to Sarina. Sarina put down the bucket, ran to him, and hugged him. They had a hurried conversation.

"That must be Joseph," Nell whispered to me. "Her older brother."

Uh-oh. Now Nell's father was striding angrily across the yard toward Sarina. He was a very big, red-faced man. His bushy side-whiskers were also red.

Nell gave out a little gasp. This meant trouble.

"You there!" Mr. Davis called out. "I don't feed you so you can make idle chit-chat. Back to work, or there'll be the devil to pay!"

I could see the fear in Sarina's face. She ran to

the bucket, without even looking back at her brother. Mr. Davis just turned on his heel and marched back into the house. Sarina followed.

Nell sat down on her bed with a plop. That was a close one!

Calvin Davis was a good father and a good provider. But he was very, very strict. I thought him quite unpleasant. Everyone was afraid of his temper—even Nell, who wasn't afraid of much. He certainly scared me half to death. Sometimes I thought that Mrs. Davis herself was afraid of him. She had a gentle nature, and was easily startled.

The only person who didn't seem to fear him was Angela. But then, she had raised him from a small boy.

Upstairs, we heard the back door bang. Sarina was hurrying into the house with her heavy bucket. It seemed Mr. Davis was going to spare her—today.

CHAPTER THREE

"S" is for Sarina

Sarina's days fell into a routine. On Tuesdays, she went to all the bedrooms and stripped off the linens. Then she carried them in a big basket to the wash house. She was glad the other slave women did the washing. The soap was harsh, and burned the hands.

Thursdays were butter-making days. Sarina pounded the dasher up and down in the churn, turning the cream into butter. The first few times, she got blisters from it. She would show me the blisters at night. Finally, she developed calluses. That was a mercy.

Then there was peeling potatoes and hauling water and all the rest of it. When all the work was done, the house slaves sat down for dinner.

After dinner, Sarina would usually play with Nell. If she was not too tired, they would play hide-and-seek, or pitch-a-penny. Or they played with me.

Nell never gave Sarina orders. She didn't like anyone doing things for her. I had seen some of Nell's friends, girls from her church. They had slaves who waited on them hand and foot. I could not see why a girl who was young and strong could not get herself a cracker.

Little by little, Sarina started to open up and talk more. She only cried a little now. At Nell's insistence, Sarina stopped calling her mistress "Miz Nell" and just called her Nell. This made Mr. Davis frown when he heard it.

Nell began to teach Sarina how to sew. In this way I got several new outfits. Some of them were sewn a little crooked. But I didn't mind.

Sometimes, Sarina was allowed to walk the

half mile to a row of tiny cabins beside the bean field. This was where Joseph lived. His cabin was shared by about a dozen other slaves. Sarina always took me along with her. On those nights, she returned in a happy mood. She and Nell would lie awake in their beds. Sarina would tell Nell about all she and I had done.

Oh, what fun we had with Joseph! There was no one to order Sarina around there. The grown-ups stuffed her with greens and johnnycakes. These were fried breads made of cornmeal, and they smelled wonderful. And on Saturday nights, there was singing and dancing. The slaves poured out of all the dreary little cabins. Someone would pull out a fiddle or a harmonica, and the fun would start. They would dance the Turkey Trot and the Mary-Jane. Joseph liked to grab me and whirl me around like a real dance partner. It was positively dizzying! I hadn't had fun like that in twenty years, at least.

Nell could not get enough of Sarina's stories. She knew very little of the field slaves' lives. She could certainly never go down there and see for herself. Probably, her father would not even like her hearing about it. But Nell was always hungry for new things.

One summer evening, Nell, Sarina, and I were in the bedroom after dinner. Sarina was sewing me a dress. Nell was reading a book. She started to giggle.

"There's a joke in that book?" Sarina asked.

"Yes," laughed Nell. "You see, there's a little mouse. And there's a lion, and—" she stopped suddenly. "I wish you could read, Sarina," she said. "Then we could read it together."

"Miz Henrietta always said no. She said, 'Book learning doesn't raise any cotton.'"

"I know," said Nell. "My father says the same thing. He says slaves must not learn to read. It's against the law. He says learning is dangerous."

"I don't see how reading and writing can be dangerous," said Sarina. "'Less you poke yourself with a pen."

They both laughed. Then Nell stopped laughing. She leaned over to Sarina. "I'm going to teach you to read and write," she whispered.

"Really? You really will?"

"Yes, I really will. You should know how. And then we can read books together."

"If your father catches us—" said Sarina.

"He won't catch us," whispered Nell. "I'm good at sneaking around him. There's lots he doesn't know about me. *Lots*."

And that was how the reading lessons began, right then and there. Nell began pointing out letters in the book. "See that snaky one?" she said. "That's S. For Sarina. And see this one? It's a T. For tree. It looks a little like a tree, right?"

They kept going, doing a little every evening. Sarina couldn't get enough. As fast as

Nell could teach her, she soaked up the letters. Every chance they could get, they worked on spelling.

Nell's father always said that the slaves were lazy, and not as smart as white people. But it was plain as day to me that this was not true. Sarina was smarter than most people I had met in my travels. And after working for twelve hard hours, she still wanted to learn more words.

The girls knew they had to be careful not to be seen. When they finished working, they hid their papers under Nell's mattress.

One Saturday night, Sarina came home all excited. "You'll never guess what!" she said to Nell.

"You're right," said Nell. "I'll never guess. So tell me."

"Joseph has fallen in love!"

"He *has*? Who with?"

"Her name is Anne. She belongs to Mr.

Crenshaw, over on the next farm. Mr. Crenshaw lended her to your father last month—"

"Lent. Go on."

"Lent her, I mean. To help pick the corn. And that's when they fell in love."

"Sarina, that's wonderful! Are they going to get married?"

"Hope so. They have to get to know each other better. And then they have to get your father and Mr. Crenshaw to say okay."

"Oh, I hope they do! A wedding! Hooray!"

I myself had never attended a wedding. The prospect was very exciting.

"Will you be a bridesmaid?" Nell asked Sarina.

"What's a bridesmaid?"

"I don't know exactly. You sort of get to help out, I think. And you get to hold flowers."

"That sounds nice. Maybe I just will."

CHAPTER FOUR

The Most Wonderful Wedding Ever

The months passed, slowly and lazily. Nell kept teaching Sarina to read. After awhile, Sarina could read most of the words in Nell's books. She could write pretty well, too. Now she spoke like the educated person she was.

One hot day, the family was having lunch on the wide front porch. I was on Nell's lap. As promised, she had begun bringing me downstairs during the day. That way Sarina could see me.

Mr. Davis was talking on and on about something that had happened the night before. A slave named Reuben had tried to escape from

Mr. Crenshaw. But he had been caught quickly. Everyone was talking about it.

Reuben had been picked up by the "paterollers." These were groups of white men who patrolled the roads every night. They were looking for any slaves who were out after dark. If a slave didn't have a pass from his owner, he was in big trouble. Reuben had no pass. He was taken right back to Mr. Crenshaw's place.

"He'll get the punishment he deserves," said Mr. Davis darkly. "He will feel the whip, for sure."

Sarina was serving dessert. Of course, she heard everything. She looked upset.

"Do you suppose he was trying to make his way up North?" asked his wife.

"Maybe so," he said. "Those Northerners—they're always meddling in Southern business. Some of them even hide our slaves. Imagine! Just because they don't have slaves anymore, they're so high and mighty. They make plenty of money from the cotton and tobacco our slaves pick. They should stay out of things here. If they want a war over the slaves, they'll get a war. And they will be sorry."

Mr. Davis was turning a bit purple. I was afraid he would explode, right at the table. I hoped he did not know I was a Northerner.

Though I had never experienced a war, I had lived long enough to know that a dangerous situation was brewing. I had been hearing both sides of this argument over slavery for my whole life. If Mr. Davis's anger was so strong, then others likely felt the same.

Sarina had not served her pudding yet, but Mrs. Davis stood up. "I'm going to my room to have a nap," she said. "I'm tired, Calvin." She turned to Sarina. "Sarina, will you please wake me up at two-thirty?" she said.

Sarina looked down, and did not speak.

"Well, what's the problem, child?" said Mrs. Davis.

"I don't know how, Ma'am," she said.

"What do you mean, how?" said Mrs. Davis. "Just look at the clock. When it's two-thirty, come and wake me up."

"Can't tell time, Ma'am," said Sarina. She kept looking at the floor.

"Oh," said Mrs. Davis. She looked startled. "Well, then. I'll have Angela do it."

That was the end of the discussion. But Nell was watching. Nell was always watching.

That very afternoon, she began teaching Sarina to tell time. During a quiet moment, Nell took Sarina into the parlor. There stood the big grandfather clock. It chimed every half hour.

"You see?" she whispered. "You can use the chimes to help you. It's almost two o'clock now. The clock will chime twice." They waited. In a moment, the clock chimed, just as Nell had said it would.

"Now, look at the hands. Big hand on the twelve, little hand on the two." Sarina had learned her numbers, so she could do that part. "Every time the clock chimes, try to run in here and look at the hands. You'll figure it out soon." They heard Angela's footsteps coming down the hallway. "I'll teach you more tomorrow," whispered Nell. Then she took me and ran upstairs.

Fall came. The weather got cooler. One Saturday night, Sarina came running home, breathless. She burst into the bedroom.

"Nell!" she cried. "Guess what?"

"I can't guess," said Nell with a laugh.

"Joseph and Anne are getting married!"

"*Really?*"

"Really. Joseph got permission from your

father. And Anne got permission from Mr. Crenshaw. So they can do it!"

"Oh, Sarina! I'm so happy for them!" said Nell. "When will they do it?"

"I don't know. Pretty soon, though."

"We have to get ready quick then. It's going to be the most wonderful wedding ever!"

Soon preparations began for the wedding. Maybe it was because Joseph was Sarina's brother, and Sarina worked in the house, but a big fuss was made. The wedding would take place on the front porch of the big house. Then there would be a party on the lawn.

Mrs. Davis found a lovely old dress of hers in a trunk. It was a fluffy white dress for tea parties. She brought it into the girls' bedroom one evening.

"What do you think about this dress?" she said. She held it up in front of her.

"It's beautiful, Ma'am!" said Sarina.

"Do you think it would make a nice wedding dress for Anne?" asked Mrs. Davis.

Sarina's eyes almost popped out.

"I believe Anne's a lot shorter than you, Mother," said Nell.

"Well, we can just cut the dress down," said Mrs. Davis. "Angela can do it."

"You would let her have it, Ma'am?" said Sarina.

"I'm not going to wear this dress again," said Nell's mother. "It's not the fashion anymore."

"It will look just beautiful on Anne," said Nell.

And so it was decided. This would be the bride's dress.

At last, the big day came.

It was on a Sunday, the slaves' day off. It was set to start after everyone had returned from church. The family got back early, in the horse

arriage. The slaves came later because they had
to walk the two miles home.

While they waited for the slaves, Nell and
Sarina finished decorating. Sarina had been
allowed to ride in the carriage so she could get
home in time to get things ready. They strung
flower garlands between the big white pillars on
the front porch. They folded all the cloth nap-
kins like big white birds, just as Angela had
taught them.

Sarina had made me a pretty white dress for
the occasion. It was made out of a stained napkin Angela had given her. Turned inside-out, the
napkin made a fine dress for me.

Sarina sat me up next to the big punch bowl
as a decoration. Then she filled my lap with wild-
flowers. I must say, I looked very nice indeed. I
only hoped no one would spill punch on me.

Sarina looked lovely, too. She was indeed
the bridesmaid. She was wearing a dress of

Nell's, and Angela had cut a huge bunch of lilies for her to carry. Angela had also braided her hair in a special way. It had little daisies wound into it.

Angela and the other house slaves had gotten up very early that morning. They had done a lot of work before it was time to leave for church. Now everything was ready. The only thing left to do was bring the food and drink from the ice house at the last minute.

At last, the slaves arrived. They came walking up the road and crossed the little bridge to the lawn, singing hymns. Joseph and Anne were at the front. They walked arm in arm.

Mr. Crenshaw and his wife pulled up in their big carriage. Mr. Crenshaw was going to perform the wedding ceremony. I had heard that slaves could not be legally married, so their owners often married them. That way, the owners felt that they were doing their Christian duty to the slaves. And of course, when the slaves got married, they had children, and the children belonged to the owners.

Now it was time to begin. The porch was so wide that it could hold everyone. Anne looked beautiful in Mrs. Davis's old dress. Angela had cut it down perfectly. The big hoop skirt stood out in the most wonderful way.

Joseph had nothing to wear but his work clothes. But he looked splendid anyhow. He was smiling very hard. He had Sarina's smile, I thought.

Mr. Crenshaw cleared his throat. "Do you, Joseph, take Anne to be your wife, for as long as you both shall live?" he said.

"Yes, Sir," said Joseph.

"Say 'I do,'" Mr. Crenshaw told him.

"I do, Sir," said Joseph.

"And do you, Anne, take Joseph to be your husband, for as long as you both shall live?"

"I do," said Anne.

Just then I felt quite angry. Mr. Crenshaw knew very well that Anne and Joseph could be sold and separated at any time. And Anne and Joseph knew it, too. Right then, it was a good thing I couldn't speak.

"Then I now pronounce you man and wife," said Mr. Crenshaw.

And that was the ceremony.

Then the fun began. The food and drink were brought out. There was fried chicken piled high. There were collard greens and sweet potatoes. And there was fruit punch in the bowl beside me. Everyone took their lunches and fanned out onto the lawn. It was a beautiful day.

Someone started playing, and others began to dance. Everyone was happy that day. Joseph danced with his new wife, and then with Sarina. Sarina danced with Nell. Even Mr. Crenshaw danced with his wife. Mr. Davis did not dance, but he sat up on the porch, beaming. He didn't care how much fun his slaves had, as long as it was on Sunday. I'd often heard him say this.

The festivities went on all afternoon. But toward evening, I caught sight of Joseph and Anne. They were standing under a cottonwood tree nearby. Anne was wiping away a tear. She would have to go home to Mr. Crenshaw's soon.

Joseph put his arms around her. "Don't worry," I heard him say. "I'll see you Saturday night. And then we'll have all day on Sundays." Then he laughed. "Besides," he said, "you'll like me better if you don't see me so much."

She smiled through her tears. "I'll try not to think about you," she said.

I hoped they would have many happy days together. But I did not yet know what was to happen to the young slave couple.

CHAPTER FIVE

Trouble and More Trouble

After the wedding, life went back to normal. Angela began teaching Sarina how to spin wool. The sheep on the farm provided all the wool for the slaves' clothes. Most of the Davises' clothes were ordered from New York or Paris.

Sarina kept on reading Nell's books. She loved *Aesop's Fables* the most.

But the best news was that Joseph and Anne were going to have a baby. Sarina was going to be an aunt! Nell could hardly have been more excited if it were her own family.

"Do you know what I'm going to do?" she said

to Sarina. "I'm going to ask my father if he would buy Anne from Mr. Crenshaw. Or maybe he could trade her for somebody else. Someone here who isn't married. That way, they could be together!"

"Oh! Do you think he would do it?" said Sarina.

"I'll have to wait until I can catch him in a good mood," Nell replied.

"That might take awhile," said Sarina. She smiled.

Dinnertimes were becoming less and less fun at the Davis home. Mr. Davis would bring the newspaper to the table. He did not like what he was reading. His face was purple more often than not.

One day in November of 1860, he slapped the paper down onto the table. "Well," he said, "they've done it now."

"Done what, dear?" asked his wife.

"They have gone and elected Mr. Lincoln president. If they want trouble, it's trouble they will get. Oh, yes, they will, by heaven!"

Nell and Sarina did not know exactly what Mr. Davis was talking about. I didn't either. But we all knew that something big was wrong in the country. And we knew that it had something to do with fighting about slaves. From the conversation in the Davis home, I understood this much: The North did not want slavery to be allowed anymore, and the South wanted to keep it. And President Lincoln was from Illinois, where there were no slaves. That meant he wanted to end slavery. And most of all, he wanted to keep the country together.

A few weeks later, Mr. Davis again slapped the paper down. "I hope they are satisfied now," he said. "Seven Southern states have left the Union. I'm sure the rest will follow soon. The country will be split in half, North and South and there will be civil war."

Mrs. Davis gasped.

"If I must fight, then I will," he continued. "Many of the men have been speaking about it. I will take one of the slaves along to care for my horse. Henry is good at it."

Now we heard Angela gasp from the kitchen. Mr. Davis was taking her son! What if Henry were killed in a war that was supposed to set him free? It was too awful.

"I'm sure this will blow over, dear," said Mrs. Davis. "It can't come to war."

"We'll see," said Mr. Davis. "We'll see."

I shivered a bit. Even a doll does not want war.

After dinner, Nell did something I had never seen her do before. When everyone had left the table, she took the newspaper. There was no rule against it. She just had never been interested efore. But I guessed that now she wanted to figre out what all this news was about.

She took the paper up to her room and was
ooking at it when Sarina came upstairs.

"What's that you have?" asked Sarina.

"It's the newspaper," said Nell. She scrunched
er face as she tried to read it.

"Is it hard to read?"

"Very hard. But I'm trying to understand
vhat Father is talking about. Here, come and see
f you can make sense of it."

Sarina sat down beside Nell. She looked at
he tiny black words and bit her lip. "Secede,"
he said. "Isn't that when you do well at somehing?"

"No, I think that's *succeed*," said Nell. "I don't
:now what that other word means."

Suddenly, the door flew all the way open
vith a bang. The girls froze. There was no time
o hide the paper.

Standing in the doorway was the worst possible person. It was Mr. Davis. He *never* came to Nell's room.

"I was just looking for my newspaper," he began saying. "Angela said you might have—"

Then he stopped cold. He looked at the two girls. He looked at the newspaper. It was being held up by one white hand and one brown hand. He took in the whole scene, very slowly. I felt as if even I looked guilty.

His face grew darker and darker purple. "Nell," he said, "have you taught this child to read?"

There was no point in lying. "Yes, Father," said Nell. "Just a little," she added.

"And do you know what the legal punishment is for a slave learning to read?" he said. His voice was getting louder now.

"No, Sir," said Nell. Sarina was too terrified to speak at all.

"It is twenty lashes of the whip!" he thundered.

I felt Sarina jump as if she had already been struck.

Now Mr. Davis lowered his voice. "Unfortunately," he said, "the girl is not the only one who is punished. If people hear about this, I will have to pay a fine. A large fine—two hundred dollars. I do not want this to cost me two hundred dollars. So we are going to forget this happened. Do you understand?" He snatched the newspaper away. "But if I ever . . . *ever* find out that you are doing this again, I will pay the fine and you will feel the lash. Both of you! So help me God!"

Then he crumpled up the newspaper and threw it aside.

Both girls were crying, and Sarina was squeezing me very, very hard.

Mr. Davis was beginning to turn away when his eye fell on me. I think it might have been the first time he had ever noticed me. But he could see how much I meant to Sarina.

"And since you like that doll so much," he said, "you will be deprived of her company. She is going into my closet!"

He tore me out of Sarina's hands and carried me off, dangling by one foot.

CHAPTER SIX

Crisis

I spent about a week in that closet. It was the darkest place in which I have ever been shut up. There was no air at all. The door did not open once, until the day Mrs. Davis finally let me out. I had never been so happy to see the sunshine!

I soon found out that I had only been rescued at the urging of Mrs. Davis. Mr. Davis was still angry. He now had little to say to either of the girls. He just glared, especially at Sarina. He even glared at me.

The girls had stopped reading together. It

was too dangerous. But at least Nell knew one thing. She had given Sarina something that could never be taken away. "You'll always know how to read and write now," she whispered to Sarina one night. "You'll never forget."

"I never will," said Sarina. "Never."

"It's not fair that you're not allowed," said Nell.

"A lot of things aren't fair, I guess," Sarina replied.

As time went on, the war became a reality. Now, there was talk of nothing else at the dinner table.

"I was speaking with Mrs. Herbert yesterday," said Mrs. Davis one summer night. "She has a sister living in Virginia. Her sister wrote her a letter last week. She said that Union troops had come in—"

"Who are the Union troops, Mother?" Nell

interrupted. She knew better than to ask her father.

"Why, they're those soldiers from up North, dear," said Mrs. Davis. "They wear blue outfits. Our boys wear gray. Anyway, a little group of Union soldiers came around to Mrs. Herbert's sister's farm. She said they were as hungry as bears. Just took whatever there was to eat. They didn't hurt anybody. They just grabbed all the food and left. They even took the chickens."

"I'd better tell the field hands to hide away some of our food," said Mr. Davis. He looked very grim.

When her chores were finished, Sarina did not go upstairs that night. Nell sat in her room, looking out the windows. "I wonder where Sarina's got to?" she said to me. Of course, I had no clue, and could not have said if I did. But I was wondering the same thing myself.

At last Sarina came in. She looked very upset.

"What's the matter?" Nell asked her.

"It's Anne's time to have the baby," said Sarina. "But Joseph's crazy with worry. He's getting news every little while. It doesn't sound good. Something isn't going right."

"Something isn't going right?" said Nell. "Like what?"

"I don't know," said Sarina. "I don't know."

Sarina picked me up and began to pace up and down the room like a lion in a cage.

"Can he go over there and be with her?" Nell asked worriedly.

"Can't. It's cotton-picking time. He'll never get a note from your father to show the paterollers. Nobody's allowed to go anywhere during cotton time."

She kept pacing. Back and forth, back and forth she went, until I was feeling dizzy.

Finally, she walked over to Nell's writing

desk. She sat down, putting me on the desk nearby.

"What are you doing?" asked Nell. She sounded really scared now.

"Never you mind," said Sarina. "What you don't know won't hurt you. You already did enough for me. I don't want you to get in trouble."

Sarina took out a piece of Nell's good writing paper. She opened the ink bottle and picked up Nell's quill pen.

Nell just stared at her, watching her write. Maybe Nell didn't know what she was writing, but I could see it plain as day.

JOSEPH HAS PERMISSION TO BE OUT AFTER DARK, she wrote. HE MUST VISIT HIS SICK WIFE. And then she signed it: CALVIN DAVIS.

Quickly, Sarina folded up the note, scooped me up, and ran out of the room.

As she ran down the stairs, she tucked the

note underneath my skirt. "Nobody will ever look under there," she whispered to me.

I must admit, I was trembling down to my pegs. I had never been a part of something this dangerous before.

Mr. Davis was reading a book in the big chair in the parlor. He looked up as Sarina hurried past him. "I hope you're not up to anything, young lady," he said warningly. He even gave me a sharp look, as if he suspected me as well.

"No, Sir," she said. "Just taking Hitty out for some fresh air."

"All right, then," he said. "But I have my eye on you." He went back to his reading.

In the kitchen, Angela was sitting at the big table, snapping beans for the next day. She looked up to see Sarina running by.

"Where are you going in such a big rush?" she asked.

"Well, I—no place," said Sarina.

"What have you got there?"

"N-Nothing," Sarina said. "Just Hitty."

"And you're taking Hitty no place with you?"

"We're just going out for a little while. We'll be back soon," said Sarina.

Angela gave her a funny look. She could read Sarina very well by now. She knew that something was going on. But she let it pass. "Just don't be back too late," she said.

"I won't," said Sarina.

Then she ran to Joseph's cabin as fast as her legs could carry her.

CHAPTER SEVEN

Joseph's Journey

All that night, Sarina lay in bed, shivering. Lying next to her, I knew what she was thinking. I shared her fears. Was Joseph's baby allright? Was Anne all right? Sometimes women died in childbirth. And would Joseph be caught by the paterollers? Would Sarina's false note be uncovered? There could be terrible punishments in store for both of them.

Nell tossed and turned in her own bed. She, too, was worrying. But there was nothing to do but wait.

Morning came. The girls were wide awake, but Angela was late in arriving. At last she came in at nine o'clock.

"Sarina," she said, "I got some bad news this morning. Your brother Joseph was caught at Crenshaw's place last night."

Sarina gasped. "What did they do to him?" she said.

"I don't know much," said Angela. "I just know they're holding on to him over there."

"What about the baby?" said Sarina.

"From what I hear, the baby's okay. So is Anne. The baby took a long time to come."

Nell and Sarina both breathed sighs of relief. "At least that much is all right," said Nell.

This was all too much for Sarina. Her eyes filled with tears. She was so worried about Joseph! My heart went out to her.

Nell jumped out of bed and began putting on her petticoat. "I'm going downstairs to see what I can find out," she said.

"You'd better eat your breakfast, young lady,"

Angela ordered Nell. "And Sarina, it's laundry day. You'll have to take the sheets off the beds. Better hop to it."

Angela had had plenty of pain and trouble in her life. She knew life would not stop for Sarina. Laundry day was laundry day.

Sarina carried me with her from room to room as she began her work. She had nobody to talk to but me. "Oh, Hitty," she whispered, "what do you think they'll do to him? And what will they do to *me*? Did they read the note? Hitty, I'm so scared!"

I wished so hard that my face could show the sympathy I felt. All I could do was hope that Sarina could feel it.

That whole day was like a bad dream, the kind that won't let you wake up. Sarina went through the day, doing her work. But all she could think about was Joseph and Anne and the baby.

Nell listened carefully for all the information she could gather. She could not find out very much. Her father and Mr. Crenshaw were trying to figure out what to do with Joseph. Mr. Davis was very angry. He wanted to bring Joseph back for his punishment. But Mr. Crenshaw was trying to talk him into trading Joseph for one of his own slaves. That way, Joseph could stay there with Anne. Mr. Crenshaw felt that happier slaves would do better work. Meanwhile, Joseph was being held in a dark cellar at Mr. Crenshaw's.

About the note, Sarina could learn nothing.

The next night, Sarina and Nell were in bed. It was very late, but they could not sleep. The wind was blowing hard. The trees were beating at the windows, making a terrible noise. It was going to rain, that was for sure.

"I wish Mr. Crenshaw could convince my

father to let him keep Joseph," said Nell. "I know you'd miss him. But at least he'd be with Anne and the baby. And I heard my father say he doesn't want to keep a slave who would run away."

Outside, an owl hooted—a long, sad sound.

"I wish I could talk to my father," Nell continued. "But you know he'd never listen to—"

"Shhh," said Sarina.

"What?" said Nell in surprise.

The owl hooted outside again.

Sarina sprang out of bed, still holding me, and flew to the window. "It's Joseph, I know it is!" she cried.

"Outside? How do you know?" said Nell.

"That's our sign. That owl hoot. We've always used it," whispered Sarina. She leaned out the window and into the wind. I strained my eyes, trying to see into the darkness.

And there, standing deep in the shadows,

was Joseph. Anne was with him, looking pale and tired. She held a small bundle wrapped in a blanket: the baby!

"Sarina!" whispered Joseph in a low voice.

"Joseph!" she answered, hardly making a sound. The wind died down, and it was quieter for a moment. "Wait there a second!"

Still carrying me, she flew noiselessly down the stairs. Everyone had gone to bed. The house was silent. She ran to the back window in the dining room. There were Joseph and Anne, just a few feet away in the darkness.

"What happened?" she whispered out the window.

"I got myself loose," he told her. "We three are heading North. Goin' to follow the river. There are people along the way who will help us, a little farther north. They'll hide us. It's called the Underground Railroad."

"Where will you go?" said Sarina. I could feel

her heart beating under her nightshirt. To me, it felt as if it was breaking from happiness and sadness and terror all at once.

"Canada," he replied.

"God will protect you," she whispered. "I know it."

Joseph moved the blanket away from the baby's tiny face so Sarina could see her. "We named her Sarina," he whispered. His sister smiled.

Now Joseph approached the window. He held something out to Sarina. She reached her hand out and took it. It was the note. "Nobody saw it," said Joseph. "I never showed it to anyone. I kept it in my shoe."

Sarina let out a deep breath.

"We got to go," whispered Joseph. "They'll be out hunting for us soon. The rain will help us, though. The dogs won't smell us so well."

"It's so dangerous!" said Sarina. "I'm scared!"

"What kind of life do we have here?" he replied. "We'll take the chance. Besides, Mr. Lincoln is going to free us. You'll see. The tide is going to turn in this war."

"I'll pray for you every second!" whispered Sarina. I knew I would be praying along with her.

Joseph and Anne raised their hands and waved. Sarina waved back. And then they were gone, into the shadows. The wind picked up again.

Sarina ran back up the stairs, quiet as a cat. When she got back to their room, Nell was standing by the window. "They're going, aren't they?" she said.

"They're going," said Sarina. "You won't tell, will you?"

"How could you say a thing like that? Of course I won't."

"Thanks," said Sarina. She knew that in Nell's place, most girls would tell.

"I know they'll be okay. I just know it," Nell said.

"So do I," said Sarina. "I can feel it in my heart." Her eyes filled with tears. "Maybe I'll never see him again," she said.

"But maybe you will," said Nell.

"In Canada," said Sarina. I didn't know quite where Canada was. But it had a nice sound to it.

The next morning, the girls and I went downstairs to discover that the world had changed overnight. The house was full of activity. Mr. Davis was rushing from room to room, giving orders. Mrs. Davis was following behind him, trying to keep up. "Get me my good boots!" he yelled. "Make sure Angela is packing up some food! And tell Henry he must get ready to leave! If he wants to say good-bye to Angela, he needs to do it now. We must be in Garysburg by morning!"

When he saw Sarina, he stopped. "Your fool brother has escaped," he thundered. "But you'll be happy to know, his timing is very good. I'll have to get him back later. Nobody has time to worry about him now."

"What has happened, Father?" Nell asked fearfully.

"The Union soldiers are getting closer," he replied. "Early this morning, our side put out a call for officers. Mr. Crenshaw and I must go to war!"

He turned back to his wife. "*Where are those boots?!*" he yelled.

In a little while, Mr. Crenshaw was at the door. He had brought one of his slaves along as well. "Best hurry it up, Calvin," he called to Mr. Davis. "We need to report to the 14th Regiment by noon tomorrow. We'll have to ride hard if we're going to make it. We'll meet some of the other men at Stone's Crossing in an hour."

"I'm just having Henry make up a bedroll for me," Mr. Davis called back.

"Better pack up a good store of biscuits, too," said Mr. Crenshaw. "Who knows when we'll get to eat again?"

Finally, they were all gone. Things had been so busy, there had been no time for the women to eat all day. Sarina had been running back and forth, getting things that her master needed. And Nell had been simply trying to stay out of the way. She sat in a corner, clutching me tightly.

The house was now strangely quiet. Mrs. Davis looked dazed. "Angela," she said, "Nell and I will take some dinner in the dining room. Sarina can help you."

Both Angela and Mrs. Davis were in a state of shock. Only Sarina seemed to be able to do anything. She put out some sandwiches while Angela stood there, staring out the window. Nell was still sitting in a corner, holding me to her chest.

Mrs. Davis sat down at the table, but she did not touch the food. She just stared at the wall. She would have to be in charge of everything at home now.

After a long while, Mrs. Davis looked over at Angela. Then she spoke. "Angela," she said, "do you want the North to win the war?"

"I suppose I do, Ma'am," said Angela. "The slaves ought to be free."

"I suppose they ought to," said Mrs. Davis. "My family up in Maryland is fighting on the other side, you know." I could see that her eyes were starting to fill with tears.

"I just hope a whole lot of people don't get killed," said Angela.

"So do I," said Mrs. Davis. "So do I. We'll have to say a prayer for Mr. Davis. And one for Henry."

"And one for Joseph and Anne and the baby," Nell whispered quietly into my ear.

By the next day, the women were trying to carry on as normally as possible. There was nothing else to do.

Mr. Randolph came to teach Nell in the morning. "Good morning, Nell," he said. "Good morning, Hitty." He tipped his hat to me.

After they finished their lesson, Mr. Randolph had something to tell Nell. "I'm afraid this will be our last lesson," he said. "I am going to live in California, out west. I am engaged to be married to a young lady out there."

I could see that Nell was trying to keep her face from falling. I knew how big a disappointment this must be for her.

"You have been a very good student," said Mr. Randolph. "I want you to keep learning as much as you can after I leave. Read about history.

History is just what happens to people. This war that has begun—it is history happening, right now. The more you learn, the more you will understand it."

"Yes, Sir," said Nell.

Then he said good-bye to her and her mother, and was gone.

"Oh, Hitty," Nell said to me when we were alone. "I suppose I shall have to find someone else when I grow up."

Nell moped around the house until Sarina was finished with her chores. They decided to take me down to the bottom of the front lawn and sew me some clothes. There was at least an hour of daylight left for sewing.

It was a beautiful day. Summer was beginning to wind down, and the heat was lifting. Nell and Sarina sat and sewed quietly, passing me back and forth to fit pieces onto me.

In the distance, there was a noise. The girls

looked up. A cloud of dust was moving toward them, down the road from the cotton fields. The noise was a bit like thunder when it is far away.

In a minute, they saw what was making the sound. It was a group of soldiers. They wore blue uniforms. They rode toward the little bridge at the bottom of the lawn. Then they stopped.

There were about eight of them. The one in the front had blond hair and a big blond mustache. He rode a black-and-white horse.

Sarina and Nell stared at the soldiers. The soldiers looked at Sarina and Nell. Then the blond soldier smiled at them.

Nell reached for Sarina's hand. Sarina squeezed it tightly. And in that instant, sitting on the wet grass, we all knew one thing for sure: The world we lived in was about to change forever. We just weren't sure how.

But there was something else that we all understood, too. Whatever happened, Nell and Sarina were never, never going to stop being friends.

About the Civil War

The Civil War lasted from 1861 until 1865. It was the most terrible war in United States history. It cost more American lives than any other war, ever.

At first, there were slaves everywhere in the American Colonies. But after the Revolutionary War ended in 1873, the Northern states began freeing their slaves. The South wanted to keep the slaves to work on its plantations, or big farms.

The Civil War was not fought only to free the millions of slaves in the South. Abraham Lincoln was also determined not to let the country split in half. During the war, the South declared itself a separate country. It had its own money and government.

In 1862, President Lincoln issued the Emancipation Proclamation. This was a promise of freedom for the slaves. But the slaves were not freed right away. Some of them were freed during the war, in places where the Union troops were winning. The rest of the slaves had to wait until the war ended. When they were set free, thousands of them died, because they had no food, shelter, or education.

And what about slaves like Joseph? A lot of them were caught and returned to their owners. But the Underground Railroad helped about 70,000 slaves get safely to Canada.